THE FIRST SNOW OF WINTER

Michaela Morgan

from the story by Graham Ralph

Illustrated by Sue Tong

This edition produced in 2001 for The Book People Ltd, Hall Wood Avenue,
Haydock, St Helens WA11 9UL by BBC Worldwide Ltd,
Woodlands, 80 Wood Lane, London W12 0TT

ISBN 0 563 55513 0

Based on the original animation *The First Snow of Winter*, produced by
Hibbert Ralph Entertainment and Link Entertainment for the BBC.
Licensed by Link Licensing.
From an original story by Graham Ralph.

Printed and bound in France by Imprimerie Pollina s.a.

In the west of Ireland, there is a beautiful place
where the river meets the sea and the mists roll in with the waves.
All sorts of birds live here – corncrake and kittywake,
redshank and greenshank, golden plover and wild swans.
And ducks live here too, flocks and flocks of ducks.

One of the youngest ducks is Sean.
This is his story.

"HaHAAAAA!"

The sky was filled with gulls scattering and screeching. Sean Duck was running amuck – again. He was up to one of his favourite tricks – scaring the gulls.

"Aww, don't do that," said his best friend Puffy, the puffin. "Gulls have feelings too…"

But Sean was already looking for another adventure.

He went to the top of the steepest, slipperiest riverbank and he was off, bumping and bouncing down, faster and faster until… he landed, skimming like a stone across the water. And found himself on the other side – beak to nose with the fierce Fox! Fox was always on the prowl and juicy ducklings were one of his favourite snacks.

"Arrgh!" shouted Sean.

Sean ran. He heard the snarls of Fox close behind him, and the snap of sharp teeth drawing closer and closer. Then he felt Fox's hot breath on his neck.

"Fly, Sean, fly!" shouted Puffy. "Ducks can fly – foxes can't!"

Sean flapped desperately. Just in time, he took off to the safety of the sky.

All Fox got was a mouthful of mud and one feather.

But Sean was not out of trouble yet. He still had his mother to deal with. She had been looking for him everywhere…

"Sean Seamus Aloishus Dermot Duck!" shouted Mrs Duck. "Just what d'you think you're doing? Do you not remember what day it is?"

"Erm… Thursday?" Sean tried, hopefully.

"Oh!" Puffy remembered. "Today is the day. The big day."

"Exactly," said Ma. "Today is the day all us birds fly south for winter. So why aren't you two little featherbrains at home, getting ready?"

"Sorry, Mrs Duck," said Puffy. With a last look at his best friend, he started to trudge off home.

"Bye, Puffy," called Sean.

Ma looked down at her youngest duck. "Now don't look so down at beak. You'll see your friend again in the spring. Hurry along. We've got a long, long way to fly… if we don't want to freeze here."

As the Duck family prepared to take off, Ma gathered them around her.

"From now on," said Ma, "we must stick together. You must all listen and do as you are told – and that means *you* as well, Sean!"

Sean was only half-listening. He was too excited about following the other birds south, to their safe winter-nesting grounds.

"Is everybody ready?" asked Ma. "We are cleared for take off! 3 2 1 – go!"

At first, Sean stayed close to his family. But it wasn't
very long before he spotted some gulls.

"Ha ha!" he thought. "I'll just give them a bit of a scare."

Sean zoomed down at the gulls. He swooped and dive-bombed them.
The gulls scattered, screeching.

"Hooray!" Sean cheered. "See what I did, Ma! Ma…?"

There was no answer. Sean looked up and all around him but he couldn't
see any of his family. The sky was almost empty.

He had been left behind.

Sean listened carefully, hoping to hear a friendly quack, but all
he could hear was a deep, distant rumbling. There was a big,
black shadow in the distance. It was getting closer.

"M-Ma?" he trembled. "Is that you?"

Suddenly, a huge metal monster burst through the clouds – heading straight for the terrified Sean!

"Go away, you big bald bully bird!" Sean shouted.

But the monster just roared even louder. It started to suck Sean into its spinning metal teeth.

"Help! H E L P!" yelled Sean. "Leave me alone!"

The struggle only lasted a few seconds. Then, as quickly as it had appeared from the clouds, the aeroplane was gone.

But Sean had been blown about so much that now he couldn't fly. Feathers scattering, he fell from the clouds, until he landed with a plop back in the water.

Anxiously, Sean looked up to the sky where his mum had been. No-one was there – not a duck or a puffin, not even a gull. All he could see was a big, empty sky.

Sean felt very small and very, very alone.

"MA!" he screamed "Come back! Don't leave me here!"

There was no reply. Only the sound of the wind in the reeds and a chill in the air.

The little duck flapped his wings and tried to fly. Ouch! His wing really hurt. He tried again. Ouch! Sean fell flat on his beak. His wing was broken.

"Looks to me like your flight has been cancelled!" said a cheery voice above him.

Sean looked up. He saw two strange feet, one fat and furry body and a big, smiling face.

"Voley the water vole, at your service," said the strange-looking animal. "I saw what happened up there and I can lend a paw. I have a couple of sure-fire, tried-and-tested, never-been-known-to-fail flying plans."

Voley gathered together some twigs and some leaves and strapped them onto the little duck's back.

"Are you sure this will work?" asked Sean.

"Sure – you're talking to one of Ireland's greatest pilots. Now just flap your feet and off you go…"

Sean flew and then… Crash! Sean fell.

"Ah," said Voley. "Time for plan B. All we need is a springy tree and…"

The little duck flew off into the air. He flew a bit further but then… Crash! He fell all the harder.

Voley picked his new friend up. "Hmm. It looks as if you won't be flying south for the winter after all," said the helpful vole. "Now what will become of you?"

Meanwhile, Mrs Duck had realised that Sean was missing. At once, she turned round and flew all the way back to where their journey had started. Now she was wandering through the reeds, flapping and calling out as she searched high and low for her youngest duckling.

"Sean… Sean..." she cried. "Where are you?"

And then she saw Fox. He was licking his lips – and he had feathers stuck to his snout. They looked very like Sean's feathers.

"My baby! My duckling!" sobbed Mrs Duck. "My poor little Sean – captured – and *eaten*… Oh, Sean! If only I'd kept you closer under my wing."

It was with a very heavy heart that Mrs Duck finally set off to catch up with the rest of her family.

If only Sean's mother had known that Sean was safe and close by – and that he was looking for her!

Day after day he searched, but he couldn't find her.

"Why the long beak?" Voley asked him, eventually. "With this little splint here, your arm will soon be better!"

"I miss my mother," Sean whispered.

Voley smiled gently and patted the sad little duck. "We all miss our mothers, lad, but yours will be back, come the spring. In the meantime, let's cheer you up…"

Voley sprang to his feet. "How about a hooley?" he asked, and he went high-kicking around the fields. "A hooley? You mean, a party?" Sean asked. Voley was too busy dancing to answer. So Sean put his worries aside and started dancing too.

Voley even persuaded the sheep to join in.

"Sure, I trained 'em meself," said Voley. "Come on, you hoofers! Get those toes twinkling… and SMILE!"

The sheep did their best. And Sean couldn't stop smiling.

"You're the kindest friend a duck could have," the little duck told Voley.

Just as the party ended, something soft and cold and wet landed on Sean's head.

"Ooh, that tickles!" laughed Sean. "What is it, Voley?"

"That's a snowflake, son," said Voley, anxiously. "And that means we've got to get busy. We have to find you some food and a warm shelter, to keep you going through the winter."

On the beach, Voley found an old boat. "Won't *that* make a perfect shelter!" he said. Sean wasn't so sure.

Sean was even less sure when he saw the food Voley had collected for him. Berries and nuts!

"Ducks don't *eat* nuts," said Sean, looking at the hazelnuts and acorns.

"They'd be nuts not to," said Voley. "You'll need to keep your strength up. It's going to be bitterly cold."

"Where did you get them?" Sean asked.

Voley looked a bit shifty. "The squirrels had some spare," he answered. In fact, Voley had been so rude to the poor squirrels that they had thrown nuts from their winter store at him. Then Voley had gathered the nuts up, and 'borrowed' them for Sean. But Voley decided to keep that a secret.

"That reminds me…" Voley dumped the nuts into Sean's arms before leaping onto a startled sheep.

"What are you doing now, Voley?" said Sean, in astonishment.

"You'll see!" Voley called. "Did I ever tell you about the time I was a cowbooooooy!" And he rode off into the distance.

Voley was soon back with a pile of wool. "I was just borrowing this to keep you snug as a bug," he explained, laughing.

With their work done, Sean and Voley started to walk back to Sean's shelter. It was then, through the trees, that Voley caught a glimpse of reddish fur. Fox was back.

"Quick, Sean!" said Voley. "Hide!"

Fox had seen them, too. Voley and Sean tried to hide beneath a tree trunk, but Fox soon sniffed them out. The friends had to run again, and as they raced through the forest, Fox was just behind.

Quick-thinking Voley had a plan. He stopped at a tall tree. "Oy, squirrels!" he shouted. "You're all a bunch of nutters! Rats with perms!"

"Him again!" thought the squirrels crossly, and they lobbed their hardest nuts at him. Showers of acorns, hazelnuts and conkers rained down. Voley and Sean hopped out of the way and it was Fox who got the full onslaught.

The two friends got away. "Voley," said Sean, "you're my hero."

But the next day, Voley had some awful news for Sean.

"Ahem," Voley began. Sean could tell something was wrong. "Now Sean, ducks are ducks. But voles are… different. Ducks are supposed to fly south for winter, but voles have to sleep right through. In fact it's well past my bedtime now…

…and I have to be going."

"No!" begged Sean. "*Voley* – please don't leave me here all alone."

"Sure, you'll be fine here." A sorry-looking Voley had already turned to go. "You've got your warm shelter to keep you from the cold, and wool to snuggle into, and all those nuts and berries…"

Voley was slowly moving away. "I'm sorry lad…" he said. "I have to go."

Voley was almost out of sight. Sean could just catch his last words. "Look out for the lambs. Lambs mean spring. And spring means…"

Voley was gone.

Sean huddled in his shelter and thought of all he had lost – his friend, Puffy, his mum and family, and now Voley, who had protected him. Surely such a small duck could never make it through the winter alone?

Around him the snow fell in flurries, faster and faster. The east wind blew bitterly. The old boat groaned as the wind buffeted it. Then there was a crack as the boat started to split and break into bits. Soon there was almost nothing left of Sean's shelter.

Lashed by snow, and with nowhere to go, the little duck set off, looking for any kind of place to hide. There were no nests to go to, or warm burrows. But he did find an old rubber boot. It was dry and warmly lined. So Sean climbed inside.

And that is where he spent his first winter night – alone in a storm, dreaming of friends, family and home.

The next morning, Sean peeped his beak out
of the top of the boot and saw that the world had
turned white. It was silent and soft, muffled under
a blanket of crisp snow.

Sean wandered through this new world,
admiring his own trail of webbed footprints and
marvelling at the strange shapes the snow made.
After a while, it almost seemed as if his eyes were
playing tricks on him. There was even one humped
shape that looked just like his old friend, Puffy.

Sean rubbed his eyes. It *was* Puffy!

Puffy was lying still as a stone, almost covered in
snow. Sean ran up to him and hugged him. But
Puffy did not move.

Sean dragged the frozen puffin back to the boot and tried to warm him up. "Wake up Puffy! Wake up, please!" he begged.

Puffy opened one tired eye. "So many birds," he muttered. "So much sea. I couldn't find my mum and dad…"

"Take it easy, Puffy," said Sean, gently. "I can look after you now."

Day after day, week after windswept week, Sean found food to feed his best friend, and wool to keep him warm.

And, from somewhere, Sean also found he had the strength to keep Puffy's spirits up.

"Keep your beak up!" he told Puffy during the long nights. "If we can just make it through these hard days, we'll have a hooley come spring. You should see me dance! I was taught by one of the best dancers in all of Ireland."

Little by little the world turned from white to grey, from brown to green.

One morning, when Sean woke up in the boot and sniffed the air, it smelt different – fresh and new. When Sean and Puffy looked out of the boot, they found a lamb looking in.

"It's spring!" yelled Sean.

The startled lamb skipped away to find his flock.

"Come back!" shouted Sean. "I'm a friend. Haven't I danced with your mother?"

"We've made it," sighed Sean. "Our parents will be back soon. Let's look for them!"
Sean's wing was still hurting him and he couldn't fly, so the little duck half-walked, half-ran towards a high, rocky clifftop. Puffy flew alongside him. At the top, the little birds eagerly scanned the skies. They looked left, then right, then left again. Then they looked behind them.

Fox was just inches away.

Sean did the only thing a duck could do. He bit Fox on the nose!

Then Sean and Puffy ran for their lives. They raced over grassland and across the beach until they spotted a boat in the harbour. The two friends scrambled across some narrow ropes and collapsed on the deck.

"We're safe," said Sean.

But he was wrong. For suddenly, with a thump, Fox landed on the deck. He had jumped after them. He was right in front of them. Behind them was a high wall. Sean and Puffy were trapped.

And then they heard a shout from above.

"Look out beloooooow!"

Sean couldn't believe his eyes. Voley was swinging towards them on a rope.

"Vole Patrol to the rescue!" cried Voley.

Voley swung towards Fox and knocked him full in the face. Fox fell to the ground, stunned.

"Oh, Voley, you came back!" Sean beamed.

"Don't I always keep my word?" Voley said. "Now make yourself scarce before that Fox wakes up…"

But Fox was already standing. He snarled at Voley.

"Leave it to me, lads," said the brave vole.

Voley didn't have a chance. Fox pounced. He seized Voley in his jaws and shook him from side to side.

"VOLEY!" screamed Sean.

Fox dropped the limp body of Voley and turned around to see who had shouted.

"Hide, Puffy!" cried Sean, and he was gone – running off down the boat, back across the rope and onto the land. He ran as fast as his webbed feet would carry him.

Sean was fast. But Fox was faster.

So when Sean came to a steep slope that led down to the river, he had no choice. Although the slope was so high it made the little duck dizzy, Sean flung himself down without hesitating.

Fox followed.

Sean bumped and bounced down the slope towards the water. He flapped more and more frantically until the splint flew off his wing and...

He took off! He could fly again!

But Fox couldn't fly.

Fox couldn't swim very well either. So it was a sad and soggy Fox that finally pulled himself from the muddy weeds and trailed off home.

The victorious Sean flew back to the boat. "I did it Voley! I beat Fox," he said.

But Voley didn't reply. Voley didn't move.

Puffy was leaning over the beaten body of the faithful vole and shaking his head sadly, but Sean didn't give up. He stroked Voley's head and rubbed his paws, and all the time he talked and talked, as if he could talk the life back into him.

"You've got to wake up, Voley! I've got so much to tell you. I can fly again. I can fly!"

No movement at all.

Then a whisker twitched. An eyelid fluttered. And a weak voice said, "Sure, didn't I tell you if you flapped your feet hard enough, one day you'd make it?"

"Voley!" Sean cried, hugging his friend with all his might.

"Mind me bones! Mind me bruises!" Voley complained.

But his voice was almost drowned out by a yelp of excitement from Puffy.

"Look! Look!" he shouted, pointing to the horizon.

Just as Voley had promised, the birds were back for spring.

Soon the air was full of the sound of beating wings and bird cries. Puffy found his parents almost straight away.

"Mine must be there, too!" Sean told Voley. He flew up to the crowded sky. There they all were: corncrakes and kittywakes, redshanks and greenshanks, golden plover and wild swans – and flocks and flocks of ducks. Sean darted in and out between them.

"Is that you, Ma? Oh, sorry. Excuse me… has anyone seen my parents? Wait! Hang on… has anyone seen my mother?"

Gradually the sky cleared. All the birds had passed by.

Sean flew back to the boat, where Voley was waiting.

"They didn't come back for me after all," he whispered.

Then, from behind a high and hazy cloud, he heard a very familiar voice.

"Why are we always the last to go and the last to return?" grumbled Mrs Duck at her family, as they straggled along at the back.

"Ma! Da! It's me!" yelled Sean.

"SEAN! I thought the fox had got you!" his mother cried, as the Duck family swooped joyfully down to the boat deck.

"Who, that old fox?" said Sean. "I sent him for a ducking! Oh Ma, the things I've done! The things I've learnt! Don't you think I'm grown up now?"

His mother smiled. "Not too grown up to come under your mother's wing, I hope," she said. Then she opened her big, soft wings and wrapped them around her dear little duckling.

Sean sighed happily. "Home at last," he said.

THE END